£3.75

1989 edition

Published by
GRANDREAMS LIMITED,
Jadwin House, 205 / 211 Kentish Town Road,
London NW5 2JU.

Printed in Spain.

ISBN 0 86227 628 4

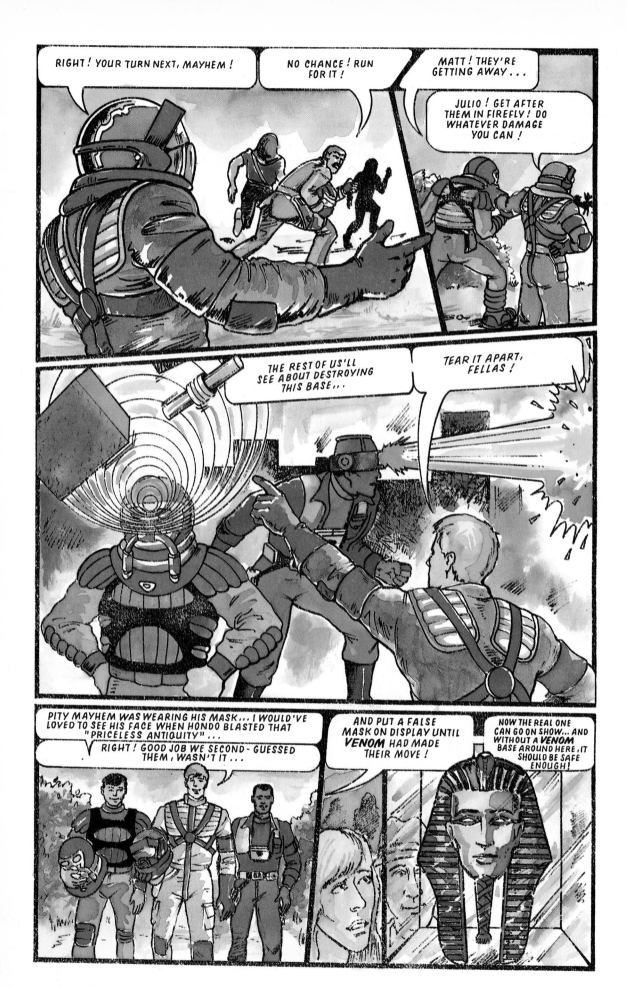

12

MASK AGENT

MATT TRAKKER

CODE NAME:	HUNTER.
AGE:	28.
MASK ACTIVITY:	Leader, tactician.
CIVILIAN ACTIVITY:	Independently wealthy. Adoptive parent to Scott. Hobbies include sky diving, car racing and any other high risk sport.
MASKS WORN:	ULTRA FLASH (with Rhino) — fires blinding flash of light to disorientate adversaries. SPECTRUM (with Thunder Hawk) — gives Trakker fre-fall abilities; creates shrill noises.
SPECIAL TRAITS:	Professional, intense and competitive, yet compassionate.

VOLCANO

All Terrain Van converts to a Hi-Rise Tracker. Armed Barrier Pod scans horizon and positions High Speed Lava Launchers. Dual Red Hot Sand Blasters are manned through sunroof by co-pilot. Metal shredders extend from hubcaps. Side exhaust pipes become mini-mortars.

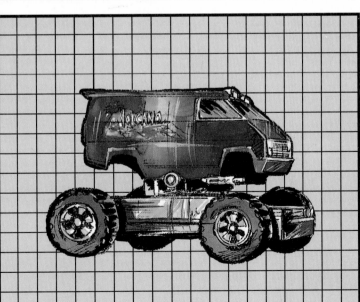

CROSSWORD

ACROSS

1 What's his name? Robot (11).
6 Rock top H.Q. (11).
9 An open fist (4).
10 __ __ __ __ __ Hayes (5).
12 Top card (3).
13 The Hawks sound friendly (6).
14 Shifty man (3).
17 14 across' surname (3).
18 High rise Mask (6).
19 He's a heel and his Mask sounds like one (8).
20 Snappy fish (7).
21 It looks nasty and messy (5).

DOWN

2 A lizard and a new VENOM (6).

3 The H.Q. Mastermind (4).
4 VENOM tanker advertises Snake __ __ __ (3).
5 and 15 MASK agent code name 'TRAILBLAZER' (7, 7).
7 A good one welcomes the guests (4).
8 MASK are on the right side of it. VENOM are not (3).
9 Wears Blaster Mask (5).
10 Mayhem thinks Dagger and Gorey are __ __ __ __ (4).
11 Scorpions have one (5).
13 Mask with a punch (7).
15 See 5 down.
16 Matt's Oriental buddy. Christian name (5).

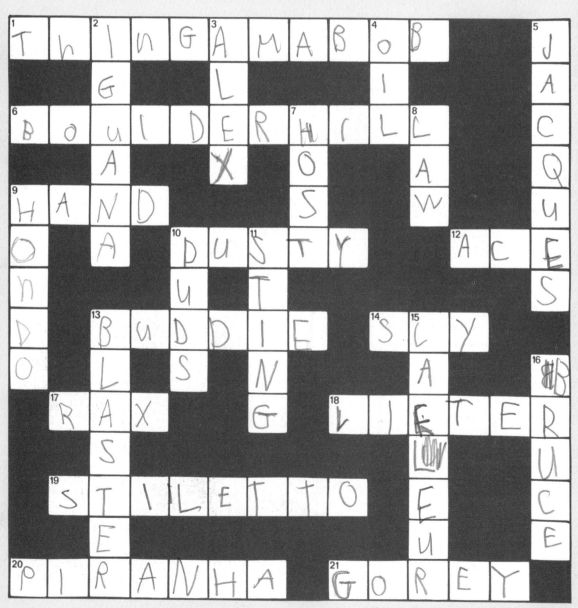

Answers on pages 62-63

VENOM AGENT

MILES MAYHEM

CODE NAME:	WOLF.
AGE:	44.
VENOM ACTIVITY:	Leader. Trakker's arch-enemy.
MASK WORN:	VIPER. Spits corrosive poison.
SPECIAL TRAITS:	Ruthless, cold blooded. Relishes the role of evil genius. Obsessed with eliminating Trakker and MASK. Possessor of a warped sense of humour, nothing is beyond his evil mind.

OUTLAW

Snake Oil Tanker converts to Mobile Headquarters for VENOM. Rattler fire Howitzer shoots long range poison pod shells. Computer command centre has dual Radar Scanners. Fanged grappling hook launches from rotating turret.

CHAPTER 1

STORM FORCE

"I don't like it, Matt," complained Alex Sector, glancing briefly at the communications screens in MASK's Boulder Hill headquarters. "It's too quiet. There hasn't been any sign of VENOM activity for days."

"Well, I like that just fine, Alex," remarked Matt Trakker with a wry smile. "But I know what you mean. Much as I wish Mayhem and his crew would just give up and go away, they're not quitters. If they've been keeping their heads down, it probably means they're planning something. And the longer we don't hear anything, the bigger that something's likely to be."

Alex nodded as Matt got to his feet and shrugged his shoulders wearily. There was a lot of responsibility attached to being the leader of the MASK team, and sometimes the periods when nothing was happening seemed even more tiring than when they were actually out fighting. At least when VENOM were on the attack there was some action to carry you through the day.

It was five o'clock in the afternoon, and Matt realised it was time for his regular call to Duane Kennedy, head of the Peaceful Nations Alliance. He opened a communications channel, and a moment later Kennedy's slightly greying features appeared before him.

"Nothing happening here, Duane," remarked Matt. "You got anything for us?"

"Not a lot," came the reply. "There's only one small thing that's worrying me, Matt. You remember we were talking about the new weather-control technology that was being developed by MacSpadden Labs? It's due for a field-trial tomorrow."

"Already?" asked Matt. "I didn't think they were that far advanced."

"They've made surprisingly good progress," Duane continued. "MacSpadden and his team are heading down to New Orleans at this moment. It seems there's a small hurricane building up in the Gulf of Mexico. It doesn't look all that dangerous — it's not expected to cross the coastline, so we thought it'd be suitable for a first test. MacSpadden and his boys are going to try to break it up. Now, the thing that worries me is that that weather-control machine's in the forefront of technology, so…"

"So you think it might be a target for VENOM and their Contraworld masters, right?" put in Matt, already turning to his computer to see which MASK agent would be most appropriate to the task. Within seconds, he had his answer.

"I'll send Dusty Hayes and Gator," Matt continued. "That'll give us some fire-power on the ground, and if necessary, he can take out the hydro-plane if there's any trouble on the Gulf itself. That should give us sufficient cover, and besides, although everything seems pretty quiet at the moment, somehow I just have a hunch that it may not stay that way for long."

"I know what you mean, Matt," nodded Duane. "Okay, we'll keep in touch."

The screen went blank. Matt spent a few minutes giving Dusty Hayes his orders and checking on the readiness of the rest of the MASK team. Then he decided to return to his office and catch up on some paperwork, leaving Alex in charge of the command centre.

It was nearly ten in the evening by the time Matt had finished working his way through a pile of reports. Deciding it was time

for a cup of coffee, he got to his feet and started to walk out of the office. Then the alarm sounded, and the next moment he was running toward the command centre.

Duane Kennedy's worried face was filling the communication screen as Matt arrived. Matt didn't like his expression. He knew it meant one thing. Trouble.

"Something's come down in the Nevada desert, Matt," Duane explained. "Not far from Las Vegas. It's not one of ours…and as far as we can tell, it isn't Contraworld's either."

"Something?" asked Matt. "What do you mean, Duane?"

"A spaceship," said Duane. "And if it's not ours or theirs, it's probably an *alien*."

"An *alien*?" exclaimed Matt. "You're kidding, Duane."

"I'm afraid not, Matt," Duane continued. "Now, obviously, whatever that thing is, we don't want Contraworld to get their hands on it. And they'll want it, you can count on that. Which means VENOM will be trying to reach it before we do."

"Right," agreed Matt. "We'll get on it straight away. I'll get back to you, Duane."

This time, Matt didn't have to consult the computer. He didn't need any help to work out that MASK would need its aerial vehicles to reach the scene of the crash in the shortest possible time; the ground vehicles could follow up afterwards. Within moments he was running to the energizer room to pick up his Spectrum mask. Then he'd be on his way in Thunder Hawk, while Alex called up Brad Turner and Julio Lopez to follow in Condor and Firefly. It was a race against time, and there wasn't even a moment to say goodbye to Scott and T-Bob.

Within five minutes, the Thunder Hawk was rising into the night sky above Boulder Hill, and Matt was plotting the most direct course toward the crash site. Whatever it was out there, at least it had crashed in the desert, where no one would have got hurt. Even so, Matt had an idea that trouble lay in store, even though he had no idea what he was going to find.

A full moon was rising in the east, shedding a silvery light over the landscape. That, at least, would make things a little easier. A few moments later, Brad and Julio radioed in. They were on their way, but a few minutes behind. With luck, they should rendezvous over the desert, just short of their destination.

Three quarters of an hour passed silently as the Thunder Hawk raced on beneath the glistening stars. Matt stared up at them thoughtfully, wondering from which, if any, the alien spaceship had come from. That was a question that might never be answered, he knew; but within fifteen minutes he'd be at the crash site.

Within five minutes, however, Matt found himself in trouble. The radar showed two blips on his tail, and he knew without checking that they couldn't be Brad or Julio. They had to be VENOM.

Matt banked to the right and put the Thunder Hawk into a long turn. The alien ship would have to wait. His first task was to make sure that VENOM didn't get there first. Priming his weapons, he prepared for the aerial dogfight to come.

Moments later, he saw them. Vanessa Warfield in Manta and Floyd Malloy on the Vampire turbo-jet. He was surprised to find that the Switchblade wasn't with them. He'd expected Miles Mayhem to be involved in a case as important as this personally. And if he wasn't here, that probably meant trouble. Either Mayhem would be approaching the crash site from a different direction, or he'd be up to some other sort of skulduggery somewhere else.

Matt radioed in a situation report to Boulder Hill, knowing that Brad and Julio would pick it up too. Then, selecting Floyd Malloy as his first target, he opened up with the wing-lasers. The odds weren't good, one against two, but he knew he had to do what he could to slow down the opposition until help arrived.

Malloy instantly took evasive action, and Matt had to admit that the man knew what he was doing when it came to flying. If anything, the Vampire was perhaps slightly more manoeuvrable than the Thunder Hawk, being

more lightly built; although Matt's more streamlined jet-car probably had the advantage in sheer speed.

Evading the first laser-attack, Malloy opened up with the Boomerang Atom Blaster, and now it was Matt's turn to make an evasive manoeuvre. As he did so, though, he almost ran into a burst of fire from the Manta. Matt pulled the Thunder Hawk's nose up sharply, turning into a tight loop and hoping to come down again and attack his enemies from above. But by the time he'd completed the manoeuvre, the two VENOM vehicles had split apart. He could read their tactics now. They were hoping that he'd go after one of the VENOM raiders, and then the other one would get on his tail and try to catch him in crossfire.

Instead, Matt pulled out of the battle and set his course for the crash site once again. With the odds stacked against him as they were, this was no time for him to be doing what VENOM wanted him to. Behind, he could see the two VENOM machines closing together once more as they took up the chase.

19

Now was the time for Matt to go into the attack again. Once more he pulled the Thunder Hawk up into a sharp loop. With the jet-car upside down at the top of its loop and facing back toward his opponents, Matt opened up with the lasers again. The Vampire and the Manta peeled off to either side to let the laser-blasts pass harmlessly between them. Matt barrelled out of the loop and came down on the Manta's tail, opening up with everything he'd got.

Vanessa Warfield hurled the Manta around the night sky, and although one or two of Matt's blasts came within a foot or so of her car, he failed to make a telling hit. Then the air all round the Thunder Hawk was full of laser-blasts, and Matt pulled the car over to one side hurriedly, dropping as he did so. He'd almost fallen into their trap and allowed them to catch him in crossfire. Once again, he pulled out of the battle and headed on toward the desert.

But the Vampire and the Manta were closer now, and the Thunder Hawk was well within range of their weaponry. Constantly taking evasive action to avoid their fire, Matt decided to try a different ploy. Plotting a

different course into the computer, he turned away, hoping to lead his pursuers away from the crash site.

The plan didn't work, however. While Floyd Malloy peeled off to follow him, he could see the Manta continuing on its previous course. If he didn't do anything to stop her, she'd reach the alien ship long before him, while he still had his hands full with the Vampire. Matt swung the Thunder Hawk around again, and found himself racing along almost side by side with the Manta. As the Vampire opened up again from behind him, Matt could see Vanessa Warfield snickering to herself. While Matt had his hands full with Malloy, there'd be nothing to stop her racing ahead and reaching their target first. It seemed as if there was nothing Matt could do to prevent it.

Then suddenly there was a new burst of laser-fire splitting the night sky, and this time it wasn't aimed at the Thunder Hawk. With a great feeling of relief, Matt realised that his dogfighting had delayed the pursuit just long enough for Julio Lopez to catch up with them in the Firefly. Now, at last, they could take on

the VENOM attackers on equal terms.

"Julio! You take Malloy on the Vampire," Matt barked into his radio. "I'll handle the Manta!"

With a brief acknowledgement, Julio hurled the Firefly into the attack, his Tripod Laser Ray slicing through the night air toward Malloy's Turbo Jet. The Vampire shot upwards suddenly into the sky and went out of Matt's sight. At least now he knew that was one problem he could leave to Julio.

Matt slowed the Thunder Hawk slightly, dropping back behind the Manta and then opening up with his lasers as soon as he had Vanessa Warfield in his sights. The VENOM agent took evasive action, and Matt suddenly realised that the way was clear before him. Hitting the accelerator hard, Matt sped on toward the alien ship. There was now every chance of him reaching his target first.

A couple of minutes later, he saw the first sign of the alien ship. In the darkness he couldn't make out exactly what shape it was, but he could see lights shining from a row of portholes which suggested that it was cigar-shaped and laying on its side on the desert sands.

Matt radioed back to Alex Sector at Boulder Hill and told him he'd found what they were looking for, but then he realised that he wasn't quite sure what to do next. His first task had been to make sure that he got there before VENOM, but he didn't have an answer to the next obvious question. How do you make contact with an alien race?

He didn't have time to ponder the question for long, because almost before he knew it, the alien ship opened fire on him. Half a dozen separate lasers lanced through the night sky toward him, followed immediately afterwards by a series of strange pale-blue energy-bolts that were like nothing he'd ever seen before.

Matt pulled out of his approach hurriedly, only to find himself flying into more laser-fire as Vanessa Warfield's Manta came up from behind. This was all he needed — caught in a crossfire with VENOM behind him and a bunch of hostile aliens in front. He banked away to the north, still pursued by the Manta, and flicked on his radio.

"This is Matt Trakker to alien spaceship!" he began, figuring that although the aliens probably wouldn't speak English, it was necessary to try to make some sort of contact, at least. "We mean you no harm! Please cease firing!"

It made no difference. The alien ship kept on blazing away with its lasers and energy bolts, and Matt gave up the radio as a bad job. Looking back, he could see the Firefly and the Vampire arriving on the scene, still duelling fiercely. It would still be some time before Brad Turner arrived in the Condor. The helicopter was considerably slower than the jet-vehicles he and Julio were flying.

Still hurling the Thunder Hawk around the sky in an attempt to keep out of trouble, Matt saw the alien ship's lasers open up toward the Firefly as well. Then he realised that there was something strange. The aliens only seemed to be firing at the MASK vehicles, not those of VENOM.

"Something here doesn't add up, Julio!" he called over the radio. "Try to give me some cover...I'm going to make an attack run on that alien ship!"

He heard Alex Sector's voice trying to cut in on the radio and make a protest about what he was doing, but there was no time to argue the point. Almost as soon as Matt turned toward the alien ship, there was a sudden blinding explosion.

Without thinking about it, Matt pulled the Thunder Hawk up and banked away. The jet-car rocked violently in the turbulence, and Matt found himself hurled through the night sky by the force of the truly massive explosion. Dazzled, he could see nothing for several seconds, and by the time his vision cleared, all that remained of the alien ship was a heap of burning wreckage, glowing white hot in the desert night.

Stunned by the unexpectedness of it all, Matt circled the blaze slowly in the Thunder Hawk, and it was only after a few moments that he realised that he was no longer under fire. The Manta and the Vampire had obviously pulled out of the battle as soon as the explosion occurred. He could still pick them up on his radar, but they were receding rapidly into the night, racing back in the same direction they'd come from. He wasn't sorry to see them go.

"Let's land and see what we can find out," Matt radioed to Julio. Then he put in another call to Alex, back at Boulder Hill. Explaining what had happened, he asked Alex to call out the rest of the team to join them in the desert. There was obviously going to be a lot of investigating to do, and he wanted Rhino, Volcano and Hurricane there to back him up.

Matt and Julio put their vehicles down on the desert sands a few hundred yards away from the blazing wreck, and they were joined a few minutes later by Brad Turner in the Condor. Donning their masks as a precautionary measure, they started to walk toward what was left of the alien ship.

"Just sorry I wasn't here in time for the fire fight, Matt!" remarked Brad as they moved closer.

"Don't worry about it," Matt told him. "But everybody keep alert. I think VENOM will probably have made a run for it, now there's no ship left for them to get their hands on. But they might come back for a sneak attack while we're down on the ground."

The wreck was still blazing fiercely, and the heat was too great for them to get much closer than about thirty yards. Whatever the reason for the explosion had been, its force had been truly colossal. It didn't seem as if there would be much of the ship left to examine, even if they could have got closer. They started to circle round it slowly.

"Matt, look over here!" called Julio, when they'd got halfway round the ship. "Some kind of footprints!"

Matt and Brad dashed over to join him. The prints were large and strange; almost triangular in shape like a frogman's flipper, over a foot long and almost eight inches wide at the toe. A line of them led away across the desert sands.

"Nothing human made that!" exclaimed Brad, staring at one of the prints. "It looks like we've got an alien on the loose!"

"Right," agreed Matt, looking at the line of prints. "And from the direction he's going, I'd say he was heading straight for Las Vegas!"

Continued on page 28

23

MASK AGENT

HONDO MACLEAR

CODE NAME:	STRIKER.
AGE:	32.
MASK ACTIVITY:	Field Lieutenant and weapons specialist.
CIVILIAN ACTIVITY:	High school history teacher.
MASK WORN:	BLASTER. Fires supersonic lasers.
SPECIAL TRAITS:	Utterly fearless. Enjoys challenge of being attacked and laughs at danger.

GATOR

(co-pilot). MASK's off-road vehicle / hydroplane is armed with a cannon mounted on the roll-bar which fires a directed energy ball that blows out electrical apparatus. The hydroplane released from the off-road vehicle is fitted with an extremely powerful water cannon. The cannon can also freeze or boil water. In addition the Gator hydroplane carries a depth charge which creates a tidal wave or whirlpool and can part water.

VENOM AGENT

SLY RAX

CODE NAME:	STINGER.
AGE:	Unknown.
VENOM ACTIVITY:	Cunning warrior and weapons expert.
MASK WORN:	STILETTO. Fires stiletto type darts and underwater harpoons.
SPECIAL TRAITS:	Loyal only to himself. Totally uncontrollable. Cunning. Smart. Potential danger to Mayhem.

PIRANHA

Cycle / sidecar that becomes a submarine. Bike is fitted with recessed machineguns in front cowling and can release a ground torpedo. Sidecar has forward mounted machine gun turrets which, when underwater, fire electric spears and energy bolts.

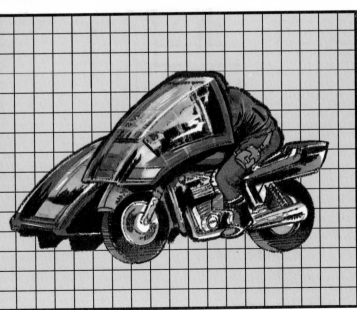

JOIN THE DOTS

...and find out which VENOM vehicle is hidden. Then colour the picture in. Answer on pages 62-63.

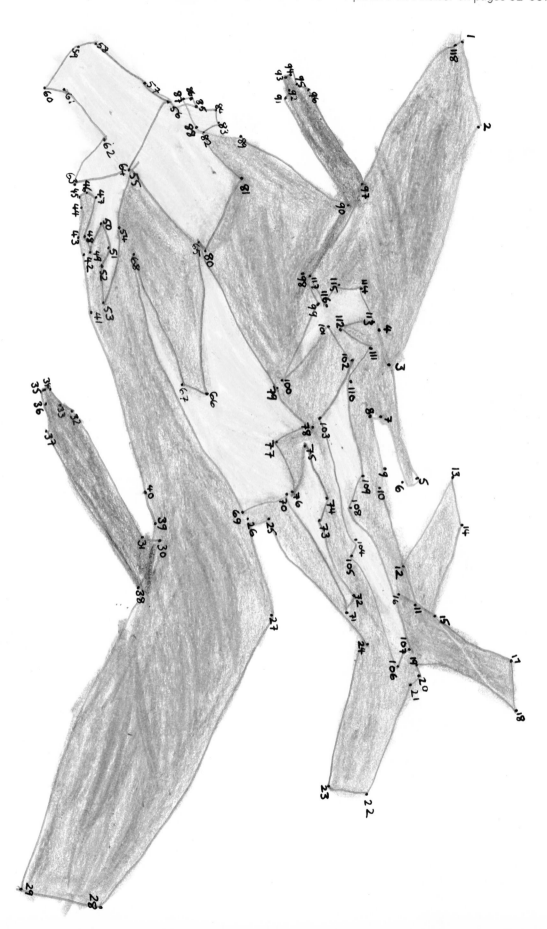

CHAPTER 2

STORM FORCE

Shiralee-Ann Brewer, a middle-aged lady who originally came from Wisconsin, arrived at the Golden Wheel Casino in Las Vegas soon after breakfast time. Like many of her friends, all of whom were obsessive gamblers like herself, she was looking forward to spending a pleasant day playing the fruit machines. Sometimes by the end of the day she'd made a loss, sometimes she was ahead. It evened out, and since her husband had died and left her a small fortune, it didn't really matter anyway. At least here in Las Vegas, the gambling capital of the world, there was always something exciting going on. And that was really all that Shiralee-Ann wanted these days — excitement.

Stepping through the front door of the casino, Shiralee-Ann found rather more excitement than she bargained for. Standing before her was some sort of alien space-monster with a hideously powerful laser-rifle in its hands. It was wearing a spacesuit that looked nothing at all like the ones she'd seen the astronauts wearing on television, covered in strange hoses and projections and funny red lights, and it seemed to have a short tail hanging down to its knees. It was wearing a bulky helmet, and through the visor she could just see that the skin on its face seemed to be covered in green scales. Then Shiralee-Ann did what any other middle-aged lady would have done in the same circumstances.

She fainted.

With barely a downward glance, the space-monster stepped over her prone body and went out in the Las Vegas sunlight. Raising its blaster, it took aim at one of the limousines in the car park and opened fire. There was an explosion, and the car burst into a fierce ball of flame. Seeming to take an innocent delight in the smoke and flame, the alien blasted another car, and then another. After a while, it moved out into the street and started firing at random, hitting buildings, signboards and lampposts, leaving a trail of havoc wherever it went. Before too long, plumes of smoke were rising everywhere throughout Las Vegas, and the sounds of screaming panic filled the air.

Fortunately, Matt Trakker and the MASK team were close at hand, having followed the alien's tracks into Las Vegas as soon as dawn broke and there was sufficient light to see by. Besides Brad and Julio, Matt had now been joined by Bruce Sato in the Rhino, Jacques LaFleur in the Volcano, and Hondo Maclean in the Hurricane. At least now they had a strong team based in the outskirts of the city which, Matt hoped, should be able to handle anything that came up.

They hadn't, however, been expecting panic on quite the scale that seemed to be gripping Las Vegas at that moment. People were fleeing everywhere, by car and on foot, desperate to get out of the city by any means they could. Only the MASK team seemed intent on going in the opposite direction, heading in toward the city centre to sort out the problem.

At Matt's order, Brad Turner converted the Condor to helicopter mode and took to the air. The Condor made an ideal spotter plane, and Brad started a circling search pattern as the other MASK vehicles fanned out and started to make their way down the city streets. Everyone knew they had to find the alien as quickly as possible so they could limit the amount of damage done. More to the point, they had to find him before anyone got killed.

"I've just seen another explosion on the western side of the city, Matt!" Brad suddenly announced over the radio. "I'll try to get closer and take a look, but it's my guess that's the direction we should be moving in."

"We're on our way!" replied Matt. Passing on the message to the rest of the team, Matt put his foot down. The Thunder Hawk leapt forward, still in sports car mode, but Matt realised that he didn't dare go too fast. It would only need one panic-stricken pedestrian to run out into the street in front of him, and he'd have a serious accident on his hands.

Turning a corner, Matt suddenly saw that the road was entirely blocked by crashed and burning cars. In any ordinary sports car, he would have had no choice but to turn back and find another route. As it was, however, he simply opened the car doors and converted them to gull wings, then hit the jets and took to the air. The Thunder Hawk skimmed up above the blazing wrecks, and then kept going upwards. Matt had decided that the quickest way to get to the western side of the city was by air. That way he could avoid any further obstructions on the road.

BTOOOOM!

Ahead of him he could see Brad Turner hovering in the Condor. He glanced down, hoping to see the other MASK vehicles on their way. But they were obviously still some way behind, picking their way through the streets.

"Julio, take to the air!" radioed Matt, then switched his attention back to the Condor. "What's the word, Brad?"

"Just seen another explosion," Brad replied. "He seems to be moving due south of my current position, Matt...hold on! It looks like we've got company! I've just spotted the Outlaw Tanker! Looks like VENOM are taking a hand!"

"It figures!" growled Matt. "With all this chaos going on, VENOM just wouldn't be able to resist exploiting the situation. Okay, Brad, you stay on spotter duty. If there's one VENOM agent here, there are bound to be more. You try to track them down and direct the rest of the guys toward them. I'll handle the alien myself."

"Right, Matt," responded Brad. "He still seems to be heading due south."

"I see the smoke," said Matt. "I've got a fix now...leave him to me...but keep me in touch about those VENOM vehicles."

Approaching the newest column of smoke, Matt found a clear stretch of road and put the Thunder Hawk down on the ground again. If the alien was on foot, there'd be little he could do from the air. Checking his Spectrum mask, he was about to get out of the car when he decided on one final check with Brad Turner.

"What've we got now, Brad?" he asked.

"Lots of trouble!" came the reply. "The Jackhammer's parked further south of your current position, Matt, although I don't see any sign of Cliff Dagger. Apart from the Outlaw Tanker, there's the Scorpion, the Piranha and the Vampire. Some of them seem to be parked, so it's my guess VENOM are out on foot...probably inside the casinos."

"Right," agreed Matt thoughtfully. "A rich town like this, reduced to chaos — it'd be easy pickings for VENOM to get in there and steal the gambling profits!"

"Hold on, Matt!" interrupted Brad. "I've just spotted Vanessa Warfield in Manta — and she seems to be heading my way!"

"Julio!" commanded Matt. "You take on the Manta...try to give Brad some cover! Anyone spotted Mayhem yet?"

The response was negative, and Matt found that worrying. This was obviously a big raid that VENOM were mounting, and it was unlike Mayhem not to be taking a hand personally. Even so, Matt tried to put his worries to the back of his mind. There was important business to get on with at that moment.

"Bruce, I'm leaving you in command," he announced. "Right now I'm heading in after that alien!"

Rounding a street corner, Matt caught a brief glimpse of the strange spacesuited figure, firing wildly down the street and reducing a lamppost to a pile of molten slag. Then the alien turned and dashed through the doorway of a large office building. Matt set off after him at a run. Overhead, he could hear the whine of jet-engines, and he knew that the aerial battle was about to be joined.

Vanessa Warfield was closing in on the comparatively slow moving Condor. However, even as she was opening up with her lasers, Brad dropped the 'copter suddenly through the air and vanished behind a casino building. Before the VENOM agent could swing her craft round for another attack she found Julio Lopez coming in from the side

in Firefly, opening up with both his lasers and his Prism Beam Launchers. Disoriented for a moment, Vanessa Warfield put the Manta into a steep climb, needing to put some distance between herself and the battle until she was able to pull herself together and launch a new attack.

Down on the ground, Bruno Shepherd had already used the Scorpion's stinger-claw to break down the office wall of the Golden Wheel casino. He was just starting to pluck the casino's safe from its mountings when he found Hondo Maclean and the Hurricane upon him. Hondo opened up with his lasers, and the Scorpion instantly dropped the heavy safe. Before Shepherd had time to return fire, Hondo fired the Gale Force Wind Howitzer. The blast hit the casino wall just above the Scorpion and the VENOM vehicle was suddenly showered with bricks and rubble. Without a second thought, Shepherd turned the Scorpion around and started retreating hurriedly down the street, Hondo was about to give chase when Vanessa Warfield dived down out of the sky in Manta, lasers blasting. Hondo threw the Hurricane into reverse to avoid the attack, raising his own lasers to return fire. But by the time he could get off a shot, the Manta had streaked away out of range. And when he returned his attention to the Scorpion, he found it had scuttled away round a corner and was no longer to be seen. Gunning the engine, Hondo set off in pursuit.

Floyd Malloy, meanwhile, was helping himself to a pile of money from the cashier's office of the now deserted Silver Moon casino, cackling wildly to himself as he stuffed the hundred dollar bills into a bag. With his back to the door, he failed to see Bruce Sato sneaking up behind him. In fact, the first thing that he knew about anyone else being there in the same room with him was when he suddenly found himself lifted bodily from the ground. Bruce used Lifter's anti-gravity beam to raise the VENOM agent up to the ceiling, then cut the power.

Malloy crashed heavily to the ground, landing on his side. The money bag flew from his hand, scattering loose bills. He made a frantic attempt to clutch a couple of bills, then opened fire with his Buckshot mask. Bruce dived for cover as the heavy metal ball-bearings shot around the room, fending off a couple of them with Lifter and avoiding the rest. While he was distracted, Malloy hurled himself through an open window and made his escape, heading back toward the Vampire. Looking down at the two bills he'd managed to grab before escaping, he found they were worth one dollar each. Disgusted, he tossed them away and leaped back onto the saddle of his cycle. This wasn't working out as well as they'd planned.

"I think we've got them on the run, Matt!" announced Bruce over the mask radio. "Most of them seem to be pulling out."

"Good!" responded Matt, following a trail of devastation through the office building toward the back door. "Keep hammering them hard! It's about time VENOM learned they can't get away with this sort of thing without trouble."

Reaching the end of the corridor, Matt found the rear doors of the building blasted off their hinges. He couldn't understand what the alien was up to. It seemed to have nothing more in mind than causing as much destruction as possible.

Matt slowed down as he reached the doorway, and it was just as well he did. He barely had time to duck as a laser-blast smashed away half the doorframe. It seemed the alien had realised it was being followed. Another laser-blast quickly followed the first.

"I think I need some assistance here, Bruce!" radioed Matt. "Who's the nearest man available?"

"Hondo," came the reply. "He'll be with you in a couple of minutes."

Matt knew he couldn't stay pinned down for that long, or the alien would simply blast away all his cover. But to retreat would mean losing touch with his target, so it looked like he'd have to go forward.

Outside the door was another car park, and a few feet away was a large truck. Hoping to distract his enemy, Matt let go a shrill siren noise from his Spectrum mask, then hurled himself through the doorway and rolled across the ground toward the truck. He just made it. Another laser-blast shot by about six inches from his feet.

"Something you ought to know, Matt," came Bruce's voice on his radio. "Alex has had a team of scientists out there at that spaceship wreck since first light. It seems they found some serial numbers on the wreckage . . . numbers that tie in to an American manufacturer. It's not an alien ship at all . . . it's a *fake*!"

"Probably a VENOM ploy!" replied Matt, getting his breath back and shifting his position to get better cover behind the truck. "That'd explain why the thing was only firing at *us*, and not at the Manta or the Vampire!"

"Which must mean that alien's a fraud as well!" radioed Hondo. "I'm here, Matt . . . at the far side of the car park. And I can see him. He's heading out through the gates and onto the street. Do you think it's Mayhem? That'd explain why we haven't seen anything of him in the rest of the action."

"I doubt it," responded Matt, breaking cover and heading toward the car park gates. "If it was Mayhem you could be sure he'd be acting with more sense . . . not just shooting things up at random!"

Arriving at the gates, Matt was joined by Hondo, and together they set off after the 'alien'. They still had to be careful, though, even if they did not know that they were dealing with a disguised VENOM agent. A blast of laser-fire sliced through the air between them, and both of them hurled themselves aside, seeking what cover they could find.

Their foe had just reached the corner of the street when Hondo opened up with the Blaster II mask. The powerful laser beams sliced into the corner of the building just above their opponent's head, sending down a shower of bricks and rubble. One of the bricks hit their foe's laser-rifle and knocked it from his hands.

"*Waah!*" yelled the 'alien' in a very recognisable voice.

"That's Cliff Dagger!" exclaimed Hondo, setting off in pursuit.

"Right!" agreed Matt. "VENOM's most brainless operative! That explains why there was no sense in the way he was shooting up the place!"

"He's heading back toward the Jackhammer," remarked Hondo as they turned the corner and saw Dagger racing down the street ahead of them. An advertising hoarding, obviously damaged in the earlier fighting, lay tumbled half across the street, and beyond that they could see the Jackhammer parked in an alley.

33

"Aim to miss, Hondo!" commanded Matt. "We'll see if we can capture him!"

Hondo fired another laser-blast a foot above Dagger's head. The VENOM agent paused and turned back toward them, tearing away some of the fake space-helmet he was wearing. Underneath was the Torch mask, and now Dagger turned the flamethrower back toward the advertising hoarding. A jet of flame roared out and the flimsy wood and boards burst into a ball of fire. Matt and Hondo hurled themselves back away from the intense heat, and before they had time to do anything else, Dagger had reached the Jackhammer and was starting the engine.

"Julio!" radioed Matt. "Get after the Jackhammer and give Dagger a hard time! As for the rest of us, we'll rendezvous on the south side of the city, back at Rhino. Then, if there's still no sign of VENOM activity, we can give the folks around here the allclear to move back in and start cleaning up this mess."

By the time the MASK team were back together, the VENOM forces had all withdrawn. Everyone seemed pleased with themselves at having driven off another VENOM attack. Only Matt remained thoughtful.

"So the whole thing was a hoax," remarked Bruce. "The spaceship crash . . . the 'alien' wandering around shooting the place up . . . it was all set up to cause the maximum amount of panic, while VENOM looted the casinos."

"It *looks* that way," agreed Matt. "But they didn't do a very good job of it. And there's still been no sign of Mayhem. I've a feeling it's much more than just raiding the casinos — as if they were trying to get all our forces out here, and divert our attention from something more important."

Before anyone else could say anything, there was a sudden communications-alarm from inside Rhino. Matt and Bruce dashed in to take the call, and found a worried looking Alex Sector on the screen.

"Bad news, Matt!" explained Alex. "Miles Mayhem struck in New Orleans a couple of hours ago, just as dawn was breaking. Caught Dusty on the hop and managed to damage the Gator . . .knocked out his communication equipment, which is why we haven't heard anything before now."

"Is he okay?" asked Matt.

"Few bruises, that's all," Alex told him. "But the bad news is, Mayhem's got hold of MacSpadden and his weather-machine. Got the lot and headed off who-knows-where?"

This was trouble, Matt knew. Glancing round toward the open door of the Rhino, he could see that clouds were suddenly gathering in the sky, and a fierce wind was starting to blow.

Continued on page 54

MASK AGENT

BRUCE SATO

CODE NAME:	MAGIC.
AGE:	27.
MASK ACTIVITY:	Mechanical design whiz kid.
CIVILIAN ACTIVITY:	Toy designer.
MASK WORN:	LIFTER — fires anti gravity beam which enables him to lift and move heavy objects.
SPECIAL TRAITS:	Trakker's closest friend, a dry wit, the true Oriental philosopher.

RHINO

Front grill converts to a power ram. Diesel smokestacks converts to 180° cannon. Rear smoke screen. Multi-Warhead Missile Launcher in sleeper cab. Ejection seat. Radar, mobile command centre capabilities. Rear of truck converts into an all terrain vehicle (ATV) with front mounted cannons.

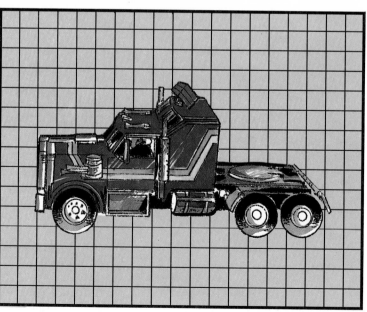

VENOM AGENT

FLOYD MALLOY

CODE NAME: BIRDMAN.

AGE: 31.

VENOM ACTIVITY: Became involved with VENOM because he was too short to join the Airforce (a childhood dream). Involved with flying vehicles, both maintenance and sabotage.

MASK WORN: BUCKSHOT. Fires ball bearings of many sizes.

SPECIAL TRAITS: Shifty, sneaky. Intelligent, and therefore dangerous. Prompted to short outbursts of uncontrolled rage.

VAMPIRE

Touring Motorcycle/Turbo Jet. Front mounted Boomerang Atom Blaster. Rear Boom Thrusters for extra turbo. Dreadwing detonators eject from Boom Thrusters.

VENOM WORD SEARCH

Can you find the 13 words listed below which are associated with VENOM in the grid provided? Answers on pages 62-63.

MAYHEM   STINGER   PIRANHA
RAX   VENOM   VAMPIRE
MALLOY   DAGGER   JACKHAMMER
SWITCHBLADE   GOREY
OUTLAW   SHEPPARD

S	L	E	T	G	F	D	A	X	Q	U	S	V	S
B	S	L	P	I	R	A	N	H	A	T	H	E	W
E	I	L	B	R	U	G	B	R	X	P	E	N	I
Q	E	F	L	T	I	G	A	P	O	U	P	T	T
V	U	S	Q	U	M	E	L	U	S	T	P	A	C
E	T	T	P	P	E	R	A	X	Q	O	A	P	H
V	G	I	L	S	G	U	V	L	M	B	R	L	B
E	P	N	I	A	M	O	C	A	X	Y	D	O	L
N	I	G	E	T	W	I	R	T	M	A	L	E	A
O	N	E	N	A	H	T	F	E	O	P	O	V	D
M	M	R	I	M	A	L	L	O	Y	B	I	O	E
Q	A	X	P	E	P	A	M	T	O	B	P	R	L
E	J	A	C	K	H	A	M	M	E	R	G	X	E
M	A	Y	H	E	M	G	A	B	L	O	W	P	N

MASK WORD SEARCH

Can you find the 12 words listed below which are associated with MASK in the grid provided? Answer on page 62-63.

SATO
TRAKKER
MACLEAN
RHINO

CONDOR
FIRECRACKER
SECTOR
BOULDER HILL

HAYES
GATOR
RAVEN
MASK

B	Z	L	O	K	C	C	O	N	D	O	R	P	O			
O	O	S	F	I	A	L	A	A	G	A	R	A	F			
U	Z	U	F	S	N	G	O	S	N	I	Z	E	I			
X	L	G	L	S	T	I	G	A	T	O	R	E	R			
D	E	R	O	D	P	E	Q	T	E	S	G	N	E			
T	U	H	S	S	E	C	T	O	R	G	I	Q	C			
M	R	R	L	I	L	R	O	E	S	P	L	O	R			
F	O	A	B	S	E	N	H	A	Y	E	S	S	A			
G	H	V	K	I	P	U	S	I	N	O	T	L	C			
R	U	E	Q	K	S	K	X	D	L	M	A	S	K			
H	C	N	P	A	E	T	D	U	G	L	A	E	E			
I	O	W	X	L	E	R	Q	V	U	X	E	P	R			
N	C	I	S	L	V	R	B	X	E	V	I	Q	A			
O	P	E	M	A	C	L	E	A	N	Y	I	G	P			

MASK AGENT

ALEX SECTOR

CODE NAME:	MEGA BYTE.
AGE:	42.
MASK ACTIVITY:	Computer expert and scientist. Engaged in planning intellectual aspects of missions.
CIVILIAN ACTIVITY:	Exotic pet store owner (snakes, cockatoos, tarantulas, etc).
MASK WORN:	JACKRABBIT. Gives the power of rocket flight.
SPECIAL TRAITS:	Sophisticated and eccentric. Always proper and disciplined.

BOULDER HILL

Operates MASK activities from Boulder Hill, MASK Headquarters.

The DUEL

43

VENOM AGENT

CLIFF DAGGER

CODE NAME: SCORCH.
AGE: 27.
VENOM ACTIVITY: Demolitions expert.
MASK WORN: THE TORCH. Flame thrower.
SPECIAL TRAITS: Crazy arsonist and mad bomber. His plots usually backfire — on himself. The enforcer; the muscle of the VENOM group. Not too bright.

JACKHAMMER

4✕4/Assault vehicle. Jackhammer has a hood which slides over the windshield to form a protective shield. Reciprocating cannons hidden behind the drop down front grill and a pop-up rear turret with 360° swivelling cannon, giving devastating all-round fire power.

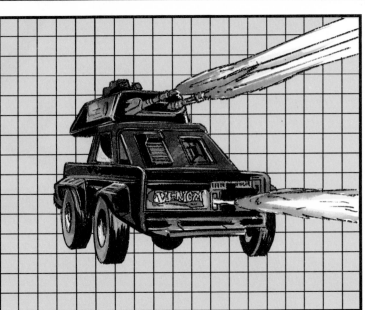

A PICTURE TO COLOUR

A PICTURE TO COLOUR

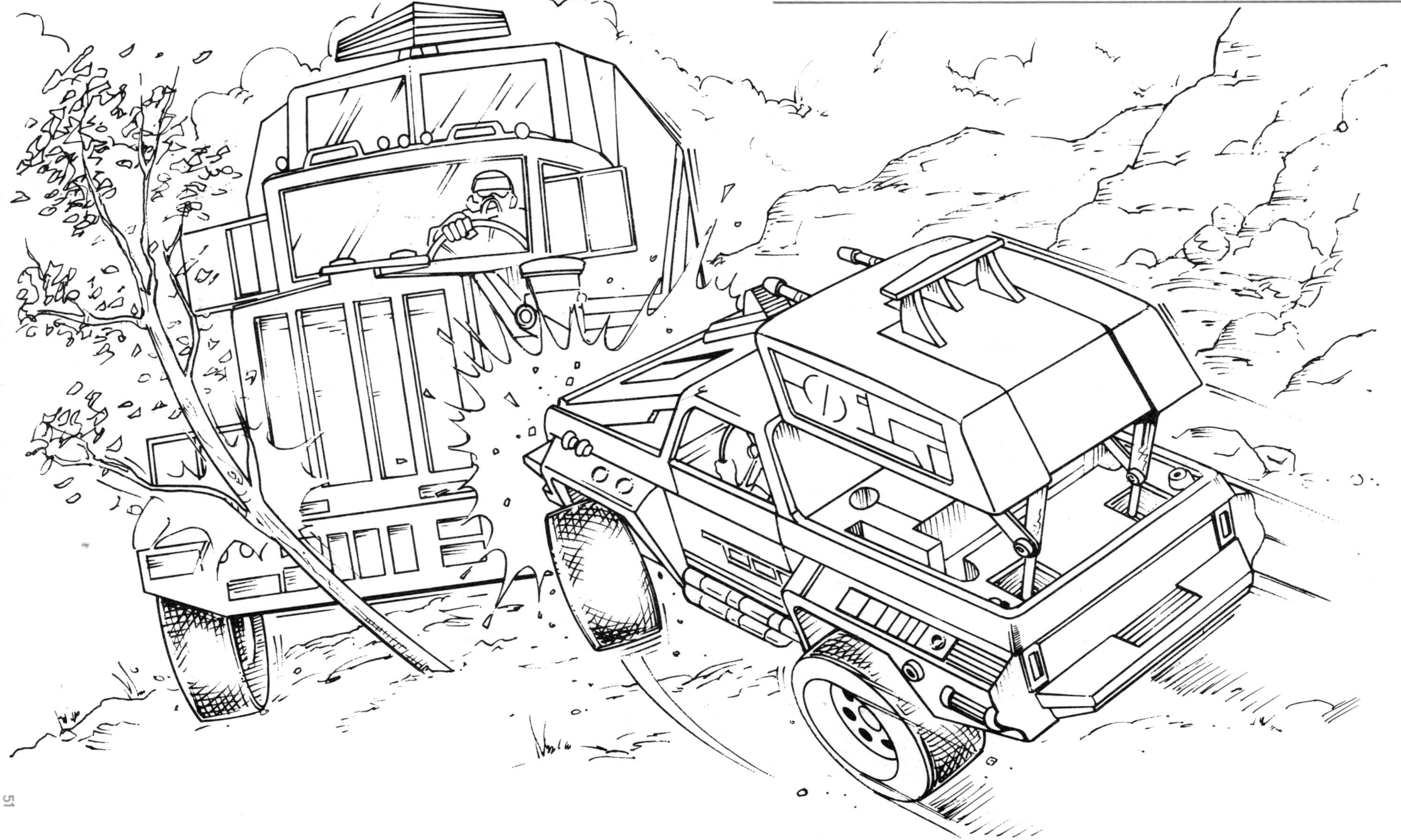

MASK AGENT

JULIO LOPEZ

CODE NAME:	DOC.
AGE:	29.
MASK ACTIVITY:	MASK medic. Expert in 13 different languages, selected for international missions.
CIVILIAN ACTIVITY:	Specialist in family medicine for government run clinic in Colorado.
SPECIAL TRAITS:	Dedicated, but plans time for maximum enjoyment. Likes word games and a good round of Monopoly or Clue with his buddies.

FIREFLY

Dune Buggy converts to Rocket Glider. Prism Beam Launchers disorientate the enemy. Front nose opens to reveal Tripod Laser Ray. Explosive charge is a Superstun Atomizer.

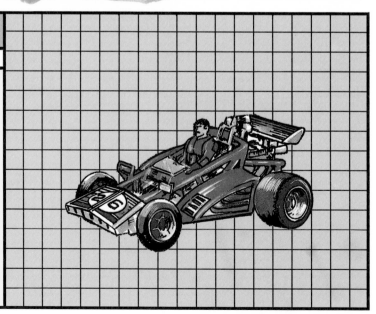

MASK MAZE

Which path leads back to Boulder Hill?
Answer on pages 62-63.

CHAPTER 3

STORM FORCE

Back at the Boulder Hill base, MASK was on full alert. VENOM's demands had come over the radio half an hour previously, delivered in person by a gloating Miles Mayhem. A hundred million dollars to be transferred to a private bank account in Switzerland by sunset, otherwise the south of the United States would be devastated by a hurricane the like of which had never been known before. Duane Kennedy had tried to negotiate and stall for time, hoping that MASK would be able to gain an extra day or two to strike back, but Mayhem had simply cut communications as soon as he'd delivered his message, and there'd been no time to argue. Meanwhile, the storm winds were continuing to gather strength.

Matt had ordered all the MASK team back to base while they tried to figure out their next step. They now had a full-strength team, except for the fact that Buddie Hawks had headed down to New Orleans to carry out repairs on the Gator. He and Dusty Hayes would rejoin the others as soon as they were able.

"Duane warned us about the weather-control machine," Matt remarked wearily to Bruce Sato and Alex Sector, as they sat discussing plans in the control room.

"You can't blame yourself, Matt," said Alex. "I would have done the same thing in sending Dusty down to New Orleans on his own. And besides, we were pretty tied up with that business in Las Vegas. There was nothing else that could be done under the circumstances."

"You're probably right," agreed Matt. "But I still don't like to feel that VENOM have managed to put one over on us! We've got to do something about this . . . and fast!"

"But how do you fight the wind?" asked Bruce. "There's nothing to strike at."

"It's not the wind we've got to fight against," said Matt. "It's MacSpadden's machine that we've got to find and destroy and that could be anywhere. Duane tells me that it's small enough to load on a truck, so they could move it wherever they like. It's probably hidden at some secret VENOM base that we don't know about . . . and that could be anywhere in the southern states."

"MacSpadden must be horrified," remarked Bruce. "He built his machine to stop storms . . . not create them! We've got to do *something*, Matt!"

"There may be a way of finding that machine," Alex remarked, turning to a computer keyboard. "Or at least of getting a rough idea of where it is. I'm punching up all the latest weather reports."

Moments later, one of the large telescreens was showing a computerised weather map of the southern states. Matt and the others looked up at the ugly spiral of the hurricane, a circling storm which spread from New Orleans in the south to Louisville, Kentucky in the north; from Tulsa in the west to Charleston in the east. There was serious flooding in Baton Rouge and hailstorms like they'd never known before in Atlanta, Georgia. The word from Washington was that the government was already thinking of declaring the entire southern seaboard a disaster area.

"Now, the thing with hurricanes is this," Alex explained. "They're circular, and no matter how hard the wind's blowing round the edges of the storm, at the centre it's fairly calm. Now it's my guess that, if VENOM are using MacSpadden's weather-machine to create the storm, it must be somewhere at the centre. So, we use the computer to put a perfect circle on the outer edge of the storm, and then find the centre of that circle."

"There!" exclaimed Bruce, as a red central dot appeared on the screen. "Between Birmingham, Alabama, and the Tennessee River!"

"It's a start, anyway," said Matt. "But even so, I doubt whether that'll pinpoint the spot much more accurately than to within, say, fifty or a hundred miles. Still, at least now we can get on the move! We'll take the entire MASK team there, and then see what we can find out when we're actually on the ground."

"On the ground's probably the way you'll have to go as well, Matt," added Alex. "To get to the eye of the storm, you're going to have to go through the hurricane force winds at the outer edges. There's no way you'll be able to fly through that. Even going by road is going to be difficult."

"You're right, Alex," agreed Matt. "Still, Julio and I will set off by air in Thunder Hawk and Firefly and only go down on the ground when the weather gets too bad. It's important we get there as soon as possible and get that machine switched off. The rest of the team'll have to follow as fast as they can by road. Meanwhile, you stay here and see if you can figure out any way of giving us a more precise fix on our target."

"Right," agreed Alex. "The first thing I'll do is get as many details as I can on how that machine works. That might give us some sort of lead."

"Okay, let's get everyone energizing their masks," said Matt. "I've a feeling we're going to need all the weaponry we can get on this mission!"

Ten minutes later, Matt and Julio were taking to the air and heading away from Boulder Hill. The wind was already quite high, and after only half an hour flying time they found themselves running into heavy rain. All around was dark, threatening cloud, and in the distance Matt could see the occasional flash of lightning. Over the whine of the engine, Matt heard the first rumbles of thunder; and all the time the wind was getting stronger.

"I'm running into heavy turbulence, Matt!" radioed Julio. "I don't think I'm going to be able to keep Firefly in the air much longer."

"Right!" agreed Matt, fighting for control as the Thunder Hawk bucked wildly in the wind. "There's an empty highway down there to our left, Julio . . . we'll put down on that and carry on from here on the ground . . . fast as we can!"

Landing wasn't easy in the high wind, and the Thunder Hawk nearly skidded off the road just after the wheels hit the ground. Matt wrestled the car back on a straight course and closed the gull-wing doors; and was quite pleased to do so as a heavy fall of hail began. It was cold and wet and unpleasant, and the lightning was streaking across the sky more and more frequently.

The further they went on, the worse it got. Trees were falling in the hurricane force winds, and they were frequently slowed by having to make diversions to avoid massive branches laying across the road. The rain and hail lashed against the windscreen, making it difficult to see, and the lightning seemed to be striking the ground more and more close to the road the further they went on. Everywhere there were signs of devastation: houses with their roofs blown off, cars crushed under fallen trees and electric power lines blown down. Their rate of progress slowed considerably, and it became a battle just to keep on driving through the catastrophically bad weather.

Matt began to seriously wonder whether they'd be able to get through, let alone have enough vehicles left to fight a full-scale battle with VENOM when they arrived at their destination.

They drove on through the storm for another two hours, and then slowly the wind began to drop. There was still rain and heavy cloud, and the thunder was rumbling everywhere, but Matt noticed that there didn't seem to be quite so many fallen trees.

"I think we're through the worst of it, Julio!" he radioed.

"Right!" came the reply, heavily muffled as the storm caused crackling electrical interference. "Through into the eye of the storm!"

Ten miles further on, with the weather growing quieter still, Matt decided to pull over to the side of the road and take stock of the situation. There were still a couple of hours until sunset, when VENOM's deadline ran out. The worst thing, Matt knew, was that the bad weather they'd seen so far was only a foretaste of what was to come. If the deadline passed without the ransom being paid, or if MASK couldn't knock out the weather-control machine before then, then Miles Mayhem would turn the machine on to full power, and then the devastation would *really* begin. Communications were still bad, but Matt decided to check back with Alex for a latest situation report.

57

"The rest of the team's still an hour behind you, Matt," came Alex's voice, almost smothered by hisses and crackles. "But I think I may have some good news on the location of your target. That weather-machine uses a great deal of electricity . . . and I've discovered that something's draining an enormous amount of energy out of the underground power lines, just north of Birmingham. I can't pinpoint it more accurately than to within a mile or two, but I'm feeding the co-ordinates through to your computer."

"Great!" exclaimed Matt. "Julio and I'll check it out straight away!"

"Now, hold on, Matt," cautioned Alex. "I seriously suggest you wait for the rest of the team to arrive, and then you can all go in together. I mean, you just don't know how much firepower VENOM will have there waiting for you!"

"You might be right," agreed Matt. "But if we wait, that means there'll be another hour of devastation . . . another hour in which people could get killed. We'll go straight in now . . . and if we don't make it, well, the rest of the team can clean up the mess after us!"

Matt looked over to where Julio was sitting in the Firefly and saw his buddy nodding in agreement. Matt checked the co-ordinates again on his on-board computer, then radioed to Julio:

"You reckon it's calmed down enough for us to take to the air again?"

"Just about," replied Julio. "Let's try it anyway."

Matt took the Thunder Hawk up, with the Firefly close behind. The weather was still bad and the wind high, but it seemed to be growing calmer the further they went on. Their course took them over the outskirts of Birmingham, and then they were closing in on their target.

As they circled round the target area, Matt noticed that it was pretty much open countryside. He was puzzled for the moment, but then he saw something on the ground below.

"Down there!" he radioed to Julio. "Near that clump of trees. It looks like some kind of big warehouse."

"Right!" responded Julio. "Just the sort of place we're looking for! Well out of the way where there aren't any prying eyes around to see if something weird's going on!"

"Okay, let's take a look!" said Matt. "I'll go down first. You can give me cover if I need it!"

58

Matt took the Thunder Hawk down, intending to make a fast run close over the roof of the building to start with. Even as he did so, however, he saw a panel in the roof sliding back, and then the Switchblade helicopter was rising into the air to meet him. With almost unbelievable speed, Mayhem converted the craft into its jet-plane mode. As the Switchblade opened up with its cannon, Matt smiled wryly to himself. If nothing else, they knew they'd come to the right place.

Matt put the Thunder Hawk into a climb, with the Switchblade on his tail. Glancing back, he saw laser-fire all around the Switchblade. Julio was giving him just the sort of covering fire he wanted, which would give the MASK leader a few seconds to reassess the situation.

Below him, he could see virtually the entire VENOM team bursting forth from the building. The Manta and the Vampire took off swiftly, intent on joining the aerial battle. On the ground, he could see the Piranha, the Scorpion and the Outlaw Tanker taking up positions to give covering fire from below. Only the Jackhammer seemed to be missing. Matt could guess what had happened. With his limited brain power, Cliff Dagger had been left on guard duty, watching over MacSpadden and his weather-machine.

On the Vampire, Floyd Malloy was going to assist Miles Mayhem in his battle with the Firefly, while Matt could see the Manta streaking toward him, lasers blazing. Rather than join battle straight away, Matt decided to do the unexpected. He put the Thunder Hawk into a steep dive and then skimmed back toward the warehouse building at tree-top height. The manoeuvre caught Bruno Shepherd by surprise, and as Matt opened fire with his lasers, he saw the Scorpion's stinger-claw melt into a tangled mass of scrap-metal. He flew over the VENOM vehicle too fast to see what other damage he'd done, but he knew he'd scored a good hit. That was one of his enemies out of the battle, at least.

Rising, he managed to get a few shots in at Floyd Malloy. The Vampire took evasive action hurriedly, which would at least give Julio a bit of breathing space. But then Vanessa Warfield was after Matt again in the Manta.

The whirling dogfight continued for several minutes, with neither side managing to score a telling hit. It was obvious to Matt that he and Julio weren't going to get anywhere on their own, and if the situation stayed as it was, it would only be a matter of time before they were both blasted out of the sky. And it would still be quite a while before any of the other MASK vehicles turned up to help them out.

"I've got an idea, Julio," radioed Matt. "I'm going to fake a crash behind those trees to the north of the building, and then I'll see if I can sneak in on foot. You try to draw off the VENOM fliers. Head back toward the edge of the storm where the weather's choppy. The cloud and rain should give you some cover . . . and whatever vehicles they're using, I'm betting that none of them'll be as good a pilot as you are."

"Okay, Matt, if you're sure you want to handle it like this," replied Julio. "But you be careful."

Matt took the Thunder Hawk toward the trees that were his target, slowing down and letting Vanessa Warfield get on his tail. He had to make this look convincing, which was probably the most dangerous part of the plan. The air around him suddenly filled with laser-fire and in fact one of the beams actually hit his wing-tip, causing minor damage. But it was just what Matt needed. Flicking a switch to make smoke pour from his rear exhaust, he set the Thunder Hawk on auto-pilot to land behind the trees, then bailed out on the blind side of the car from Vanessa Warfield. The Spectrum mask's free-fall powers would allow him to make a gentle descent to the ground.

As he landed, he saw the Manta do a fast victory-roll before it sped off to join Mayhem and Malloy in pursuit of the Firefly. So far so

good, he thought, taking cover behind some bushes. None of the VENOM agents seemed to be coming to look for him, so he guessed no one had seen him bailing out. He set off at a run toward the rear door of the warehouse. Moments later he was inside. The sound of raised voices soon told him where he wanted to go.

"Make it work!" Cliff Dagger was shouting.

"I can't!" replied a voice which Matt guessed had to be MacSpadden. "I don't know what's gone wrong! It just isn't working any more!"

Coming from behind them, Matt could see MacSpadden, a small balding man in his fifties, crouching over the gleaming weather-machine, with Dagger standing threateningly at his shoulder. Setting off a shrill shrieking noise from his Spectrum mask, Matt leaped to the attack.

Before Dagger had a chance to react, Matt grabbed his shoulder and turned him round, then hit him with two powerful body-punches to the solar plexus. As Dagger bent double, gasping for breath, Matt grabbed the Torch mask and tore it away from the VENOM agent's head. Groaning in pain and suddenly finding himself weaponless, Dagger did the only thing he could think of. He made a run for it.

"I told *him*, I can't *do* anything!" protested MacSpadden, turning to face the masked newcomer.

"You've got it wrong, professor," Matt replied. "I'm not with VENOM, I'm with MASK! I'm here to rescue you — and knock out that machine of yours before it does any more damage."

"Destroy it, you mean?" asked MacSpadden in horror. "But it's my life's work."

"Can't be helped," Matt explained. "As soon as Dagger raises the alarm, the other VENOM agents'll be in here, and we'll have lost everything."

It didn't turn out like that, however. Moments later, Matt heard Bruce Sato's voice on his mask radio.

"Matt, are you okay? We're outside . . . we made better time than we thought . . . and we're giving VENOM a pasting out here! Since that weather — machine stopped working, they don't seem to have any heart left for the fight. In fact, they're pulling out right now!"

"Great!" exclaimed Matt. "Give them everything you've got, Bruce! I'm bringing out Professor MacSpadden now . . . we'll see you outside."

By the time they had got out of the building, the battle was all over, and Bruce was bringing the Rhino over to join them. As soon as Matt was aboard, he put a call through to Alex, back at Boulder Hill.

"We've done it, Alex!" he began. "Professor MacSpadden and the weather-machine are back in our hands, and VENOM's in full retreat. Only one thing I don't understand — the machine stopped working just before we got here."

"I can explain that, Matt," grinned Alex. "Remember I told you I'd pin-pointed their location because there was a power-drain from the underground cables? Well, when I realised what was happening, I got on to the Alabama State generating board and persuaded them to cut the power to the entire state of Alabama for an hour. To put it simply, I just pulled the plug out of that machine!"

Matt grinned and looked toward the sky. Outside, the weather was clearing already. A few minutes later, the sun came out.

ANSWERS

CROSSWORD

SWITCHBLADE

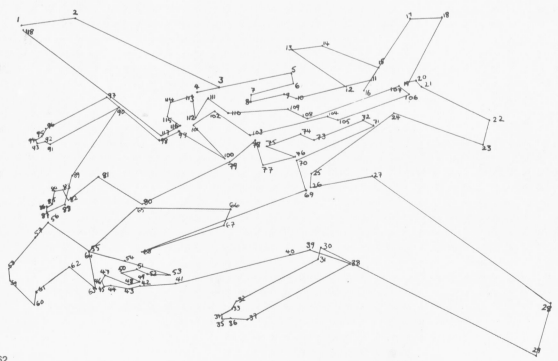